Merry Christmas, What's Your Name

by Bernice Chardiet and Grace Maccarone
pictures by C Brian Karas

SCHOLASTIC INC.

New York   Toronto   London   Auckland   Sydney

To my school friends
Lois, Pam, and Robert
G.M.

To Simon and Jon—with love
B.C.

To Christopher, Benjamin,
Nanette, and Amanda
G.B.K.

Text copyright © 1990 by Grace Maccarone
and
Bernice Chardiet.
Illustrations copyright © 1990 by G. Brian Karas.
All rights reserved. Published by Scholastic Inc.
Produced by Chardiet Unlimited, Inc.

ISBN 0-590-43306-7

12 11 10 9 8 7 6 5 4 3 2 1   0 1 2 3 4 5/9

Printed in U.S.A.   8

First Scholastic printing, November 1990

The crossing-guard blew her whistle.
Boys and girls waited behind her.
It was a cold day.
Tomorrow would be the first day of winter.
Christmas was only four days away.

Bunny Rabissi hopped up and down to
keep warm.
Someone pulled her scarf, then whispered
in her ear.
"Go home and eat some carrots,
Bunny Rabbit."
That Raymond Tally!
He was always teasing Bunny about
her name. She hated it.
Bunny had to do something. But what?

The next morning, Bunny had an idea.
"Bunny, it's time to get up,"
her mother called.
But Bunny did not get up.
"Bunny, are you awake? Answer me!"
But Bunny did not answer.

Mrs. Rabissi went to Bunny's room.
"What's the matter?" she asked. "Why
didn't you answer?"
"I'm not Bunny anymore. I've changed
my name to Daisy."

"Really?" her mother said. "Well, Daisy,
you'd better get up and get ready or
you'll be late for school, and I'll be late
for work."

At school, Daisy-Bunny found a picture
of a rabbit on her desk.
She knew who it was from.
But she didn't care anymore.

She crumpled up the picture and stuffed
it in the back of her desk.

At lunchtime, Brenda asked Bunny,
"Why did Ms. Darcy call you Daisy?"
"I've changed my name. My mother wrote
Ms. Darcy a note about it."
"Lucky duck," said John.

Just then, Raymond came along.
Daisy-Bunny put her nose in the air.
"Hello, Johhhn," Raymond said.
John ignored him.
"A john is a toilet," Raymond said.
"But my name isn't John anymore.
It's Jim!"

"Keep quiet, Raymond," Brenda said.
Raymond laughed as he walked away.
"Look who's talking, Brenda Bolenda!"
"Did you hear what he called me?"
Brenda asked.
She didn't like it one bit.

That afternoon, Ms. Darcy asked, "Who
will go to the calendar and mark off
the shortest day of the year?"
Half of the class raised their hands.
Ms. Darcy called on Cynthia.
Much to her surprise, two girls ran
to the front of the room.
Cynthia glared at Brenda, who got
there first.

"The first day of winter is the shortest
day of the year," Brenda said.
Ms. Darcy looked confused.
"Yes, that's right, Brenda," she said,
"but I called on Cynthia."
"My name is Cynthia now," Cynthia-Brenda
said. "I just changed it!"
The real Cynthia gave Cynthia-Brenda
a mean look. And both girls sat down.

"Copycat! Copycat!" the real Cynthia
called to Cynthia-Brenda after school.
"Stop that," Cynthia-Brenda said.
But the real Cynthia would not stop.
"Copycat! Copycat!"
Cynthia-Brenda chased the real Cynthia
until she caught a braid.
"You pulled my hair," the real Cynthia
cried. "I'm telling!"

Cynthia-Brenda knew she was in trouble
as soon as she got home.
Her mother had an angry look on her face.
"I just spoke to Cynthia's mother," she said.
"I want you to call Cynthia to apologize
right now."
"No way!" Cynthia-Brenda said.
"Then go to your room," her mother said.
"And don't come down until you're ready
to say you're sorry."

Cynthia-Brenda had to go straight
to her room.

At dinnertime, she was still there.
"I'll never apologize," Cynthia-Brenda
yelled, "not even if I starve to death."

Just then Cynthia-Brenda's little brother,
Truman, opened her door.
"We're having fried chicken," he said.
"Go away," Cynthia-Brenda said.
A few minutes later Truman was back.
"And mashed potatoes. Yum-yum."
Cynthia-Brenda tossed a pillow
at Truman, but she missed.
"And chocolate layer cake
for dessert!" he yelled.
That was the last straw!
"I can't take it anymore!"
Cynthia-Brenda said.
"I'll apologize!"

Cynthia-Brenda picked up the telephone and called Cynthia.

"Oh, hello, Brenda," the real Cynthia said in a whiny voice. "And what do you have to say for yourself?"

Brenda talked as fast as she could.

"You can have your stupid name back.
I don't want it anyway. I'm sorry I pulled
your braid. Good-bye!"

Brenda was still angry as she ate
her dinner.
"I hate the name Brenda!"
"It's a good name," her father said.
"You should like it because it's yours."
"What are you going to call yourself
now?" Truman asked.
"I don't know yet," said Brenda.

"What about Morris?" Truman said.

"That's dumb. Morris is a boy's name and I don't like it. And I don't like your name either," Brenda said.

"Who cares?" said Truman. "I changed my name to Ed."

The phone rang.
Brenda went to get it.
"Hello, it's Daisy. Is Cynthia there?"
"You must have the wrong number,"
Brenda said, and she hung up.
The phone rang again.

"It's me, Daisy, who used to be Bunny,
and I'm calling Cynthia, who used to be
Brenda."

"I'm not Cynthia anymore," Brenda said.
Then she had a great idea. "I'm Barbara.
But you can call me Barbie."

"Oh, all right," Daisy-Bunny said, wishing
she had thought of the name Barbie first.

The next day, the boys and girls gave
holiday cards to each other.
Jim, who used to be John, was chosen
to give them out.
It was very confusing because no one
could remember who was named
what anymore.
Even Cynthia had changed her name.
Now she was Crystal.
The only one who didn't change his name
was Raymond.

NORTH POLE
MAIL

"Raymond Allen Tally, this card is for you," Jim-John said.

Then Jim-John noticed something.

"Raymond Allen Tally's initials are R.A.T.! Raymond is a rat!"

Everyone whispered, "Raymond is a rat! Raymond is a rat!" until Ms. Darcy told the class to settle down.

Barbie-Brenda raced home from school.
She was glad she wasn't in trouble again.
She wanted to look for her presents
under the tree.
She wanted to feel the smooth paper
and shake the boxes and guess what
was inside.
Then she thought of something.
The presents were all for Brenda.
There would not be a single present
for Barbie.
Changing names was a terrible mistake!

Brenda had to tell the others right away.

So that night, Barbie went back
to being Brenda.
Ed went back to being Truman.
Daisy went back to being Bunny.
Jim went back to being John.
And Crystal went back to being Cynthia.

But Raymond Allen Tally was still R.A.T.!